We Love You, Mr. Panda
Te amamos, Sr. Panda

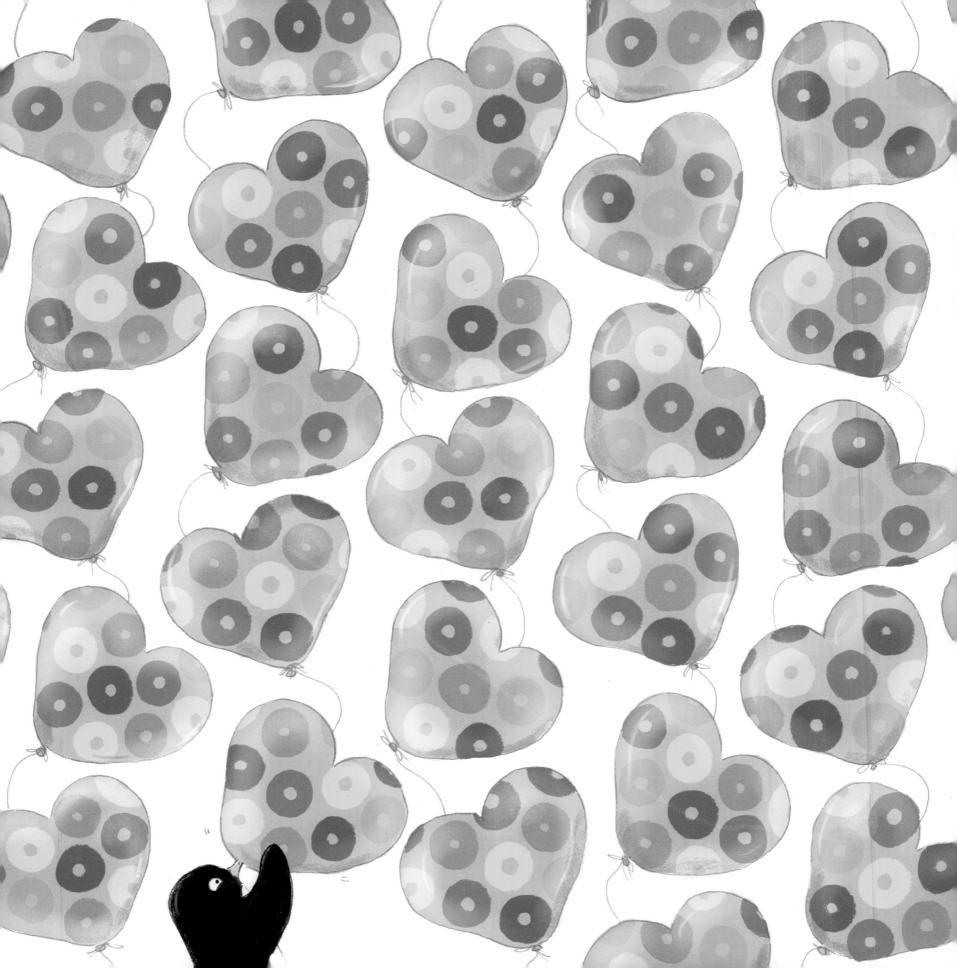

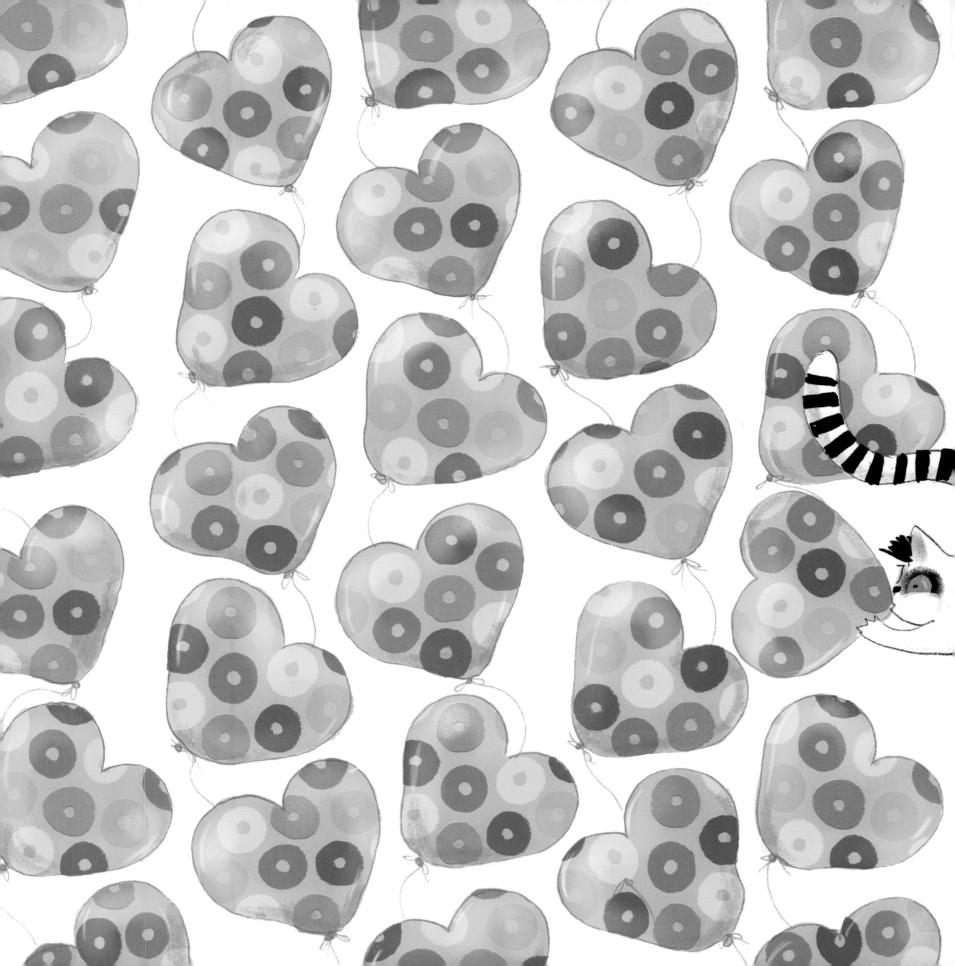

For Richard and Gabrielė
Para Richard y Gabrielė

Originally published in English in the UK by Hodder Children's Books, an imprint of
Hachette Children's Group, part of Hodder & Stoughton, in 2019 as *We Love You, Mr Panda*.

Copyright © 2019 by Steve Antony
Translation copyright © 2021 by Scholastic Inc.

ISBN 978-1-338-67002-8

10 9 8 7 6 5 4 3 2 1   21 22 23 24 25

Printed in the U.S.A. 141
First bilingual edition, 2021

The drawings in this book were created with pencils and graphite sticks. Because of his red-green
color blindness, Steve Antony usually sticks to a limited or abstract color palette.

We Love You, Mr. Panda
Te amamos, Sr. Panda

Steve Antony

Scholastic Inc.

I need a hug.

Necesito un abrazo.

OK, Skunk. Let's have a hug.

Está bien, Zorrillo. Te daré un abrazo.

FREE
HUGS

ABRAZOS
GRATIS

I love you, too.

Yo también te amo.

I was talking to Croc.
I love you, Croc.

Estaba hablando con Coco.
Te amo, Coco.

May I please have a hug?

¿Puedes darme un abrazo, por favor?

OK, Elephant. Let's have a hug.

Está bien, Elefante. Te daré un abrazo.

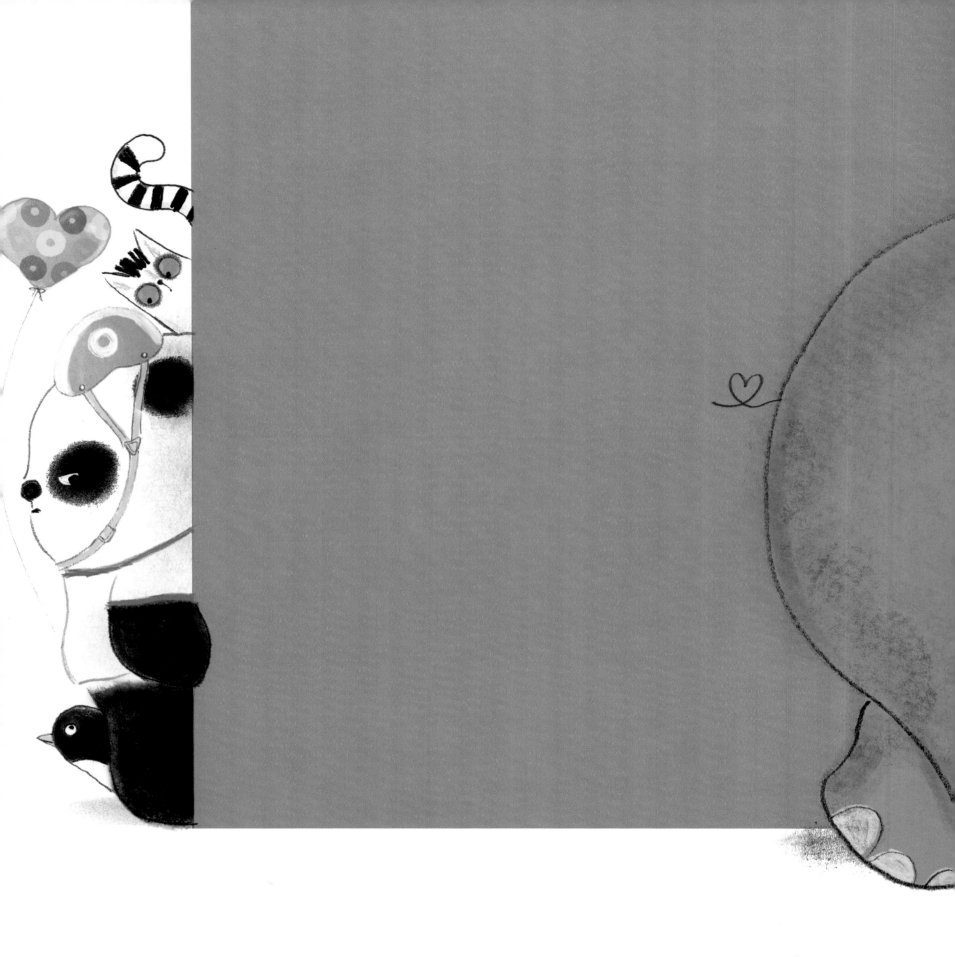

I was talking to Mouse. I love you, Mouse.

Estaba hablando con Ratón. Te amo, Ratón.

I love you, too.

Yo también te amo.

Would you like a hug, Sloth?

¿Quieres que te dé un abrazo, Perezoso?

No thanks, Mr. Panda.
I can hug myself.

No, gracias, Sr. Panda.
Puedo abrazarme solo.

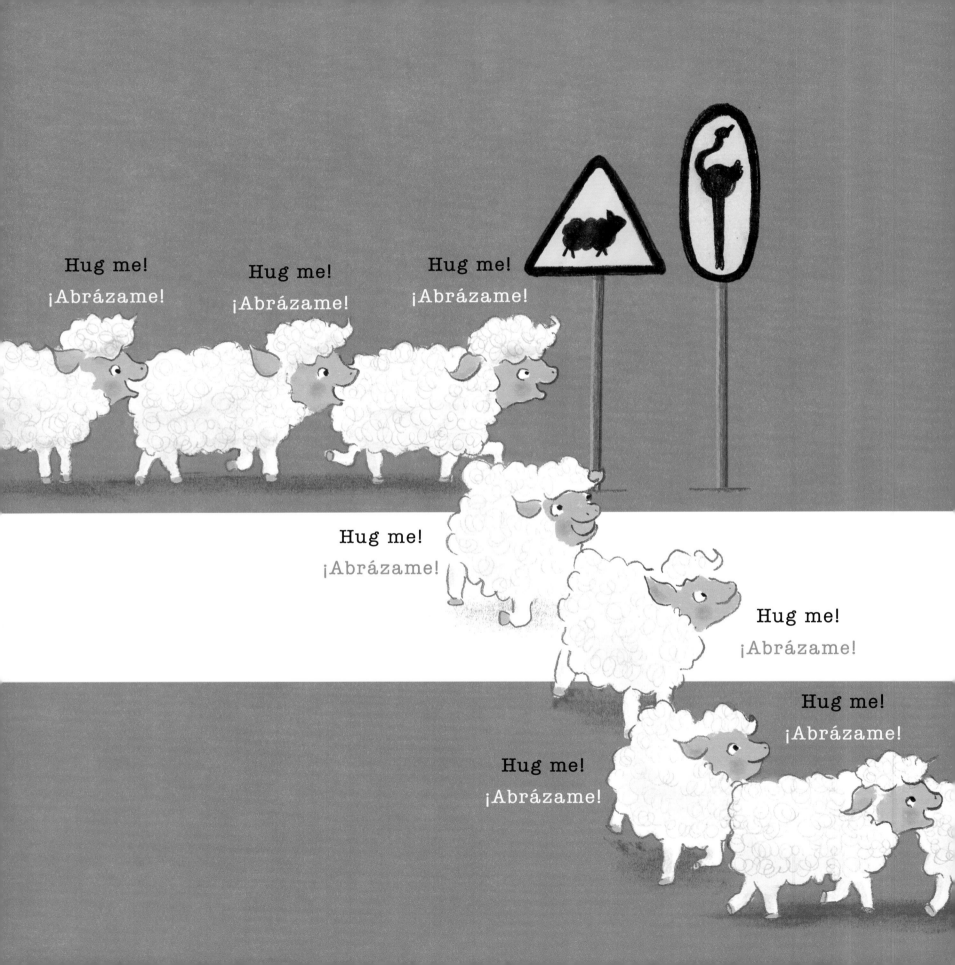

OK, sheep. Let's have a hug.

Está bien, ovejas. Les daré un abrazo.

Hug me!

¡Abrázame!

Hug me!

¡Abrázame!

Hug me!

¡Abrázame!

Hug me!

¡Abrázame!

Hug me!

¡Abrázame!

H

¡Ab

We were talking to Ostrich.
We love you, Ostrich.

Estábamos hablando con Avestruz.
Te amamos, Avestruz.

I love you all, too.

Yo también las amo a todas.

I guess nobody
Supongo que nadie

wants my hugs . . .
quiere que lo abrace...

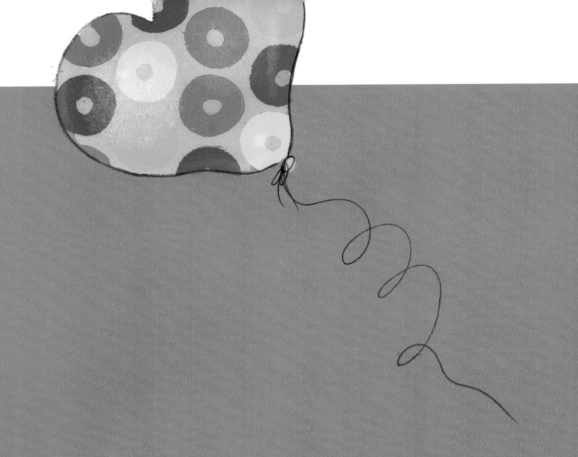

Don't go, Mr. Panda.

No te vayas, Sr. Panda.

Would **YOU** like a hug?

¿**TE** gustaría que te abracemos?

No, I would not like a hug . . .

No, no me gustaría que me abracen...

. . . I would LOVE a hug. Thank you.

Me ENCANTARÍA que me abracen. Gracias.

And so would we!

¡Y nosotros también!

We love you, Mr. Panda!

¡Te amamos, Sr. Panda!

I love you, too.

Yo también los amo.